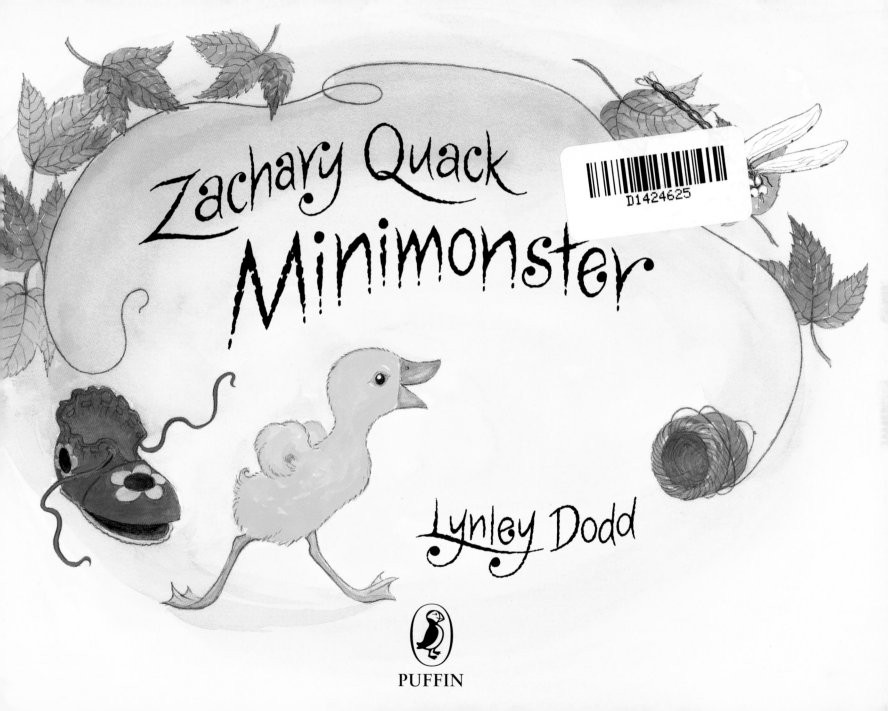

Zachary Quack
Minimonster

Lynley Dodd

PUFFIN

Climbing the river bank
on to the track,
went pittery pattery
Zachary Quack.

He scruffled a centipede
out of its house,
he pestered a spider
and ruffled a mouse.

He bustled a beetle,
asleep on a chair,
and hustled a dragonfly
into the air.

FLICK
went the dragonfly,
FLICK FLICK FLICK,
here, there and everywhere,
quick,
quick,
quick.

Over the path
and the rockery too,

over some paint
and a bottle of glue.

FLICK
went the dragonfly,
FLICK FLICK FLICK,
here, there and everywhere,
quick,
quick,
quick.

Through the petunias,
pumpkins and peas,

over the rake
and a mountain of leaves.

FLICK
went the dragonfly,
FLICK FLICK FLICK,
here, there and everywhere,
quick,
quick,
quick.

Over the sandpit,
around the old swing,

the netting and potting mix,
tied up with string.

FLICK
went the dragonfly,
FLICK FLICK FLICK,

back to the river bank,
quick,
quick,

QUICK!

PUFFIN BOOKS

Published by the Penguin Group: London, New York, Australia,
Canada, India, Ireland, New Zealand and South Africa
Penguin Books Ltd, Registered Offices:
80 Strand, London WC2R 0RL, England

puffinbooks.com

First published in New Zealand by Mallinson Rendel Publishers Limited 2005
Published in Great Britain in Puffin Books 2005
Published in paperback 2006
Published in this edition 2012
001 – 10 9 8 7 6 5 4 3 2 1
Text and illustrations copyright © Lynley Dodd, 2005

Made and printed in China
ISBN: 978–0–718–19541–0